AUTHOR'S

A word of caution for anyone about to read this book. *"Mermaid Tattoos"* is a work of fiction. The characters are mythical creatures, and the plot line is a metaphor. That said, I feel it is best to give a warning - the story ahead is not a happy one, and delves into subject matters which some may find difficult to read. I wrote this book to give a voice for those who needed one, but I understand that not everybody will find comfort in this story. To you, I wish all the best, and encourage you to put this book down.

I've had to think long and hard about what to write here. To explain why I felt the need to make this book. Inspiration came from older fairytales told by the Brothers Grimm. Dark, grotesque, even disturbing tales which were meant to frighten and impart lessons to the younger generation.

I have been asked who this book is for, and I intended it to be for all ages. I don't feel that there is anything in this book that is darker than a story where a stepmother eats what she thinks is her stepdaughter's heart, or where two women cut off bits of their feet in order to fit into shoes, or where a wolf devours an old woman, and lays in wait for her granddaughter.

But there may be those who disagree with that sentiment. To them, I say that there will be some who read this book and see only a story about a mermaid who is branded by pirates. And others will read this story and know exactly what it is about.

They are the ones who this book is for.

ISBN Number: 979-8-9923256-2-1
"Mermaid Tattoos" written and illustrated by Angela Flatt
Edited by Philomena Sherwood
Audiobook narration by Mina Rose

Audiobook version found here:

Copyright © 2024 by Angela Flatt

All rights reserved.

No portion of this book may be reproduced in any form without written permission from the publisher or author, except as permitted by U.S. copyright law.

"AquaReal - Realistic Watercolor" brushes by Lisa Glanz
"Cave" and "Underwater" stamps by Rinki
"Under the Sea" brushes by Sandra Winther Art
"Water Brush" procreate set by bybaobob
"Mini set Watercolor" brushes by Manero Brushes
"Clouds Brush" pack by Devin Elle Kurtz

For the mermaids

Once upon a time, in the very depths of the ocean, there was a mermaid. Her name was Mara.

She lived in the ocean with her family. She had lots of animal friends, including a pair of dolphins, and a starfish which perched in her hair. Whenever she traveled to the surface, she always made sure to feed traveling seagulls.

Mara's family was never brave enough to join her at the surface. Her siblings were particularly curious, but their parents warned them about being spotted by humans.
Mara, however, was always cautious.
She would hide among the
rocks or swim alongside her dolphins as camouflage.

She loved watching what the humans were doing inside of their ships. Sometimes, she saw men carrying many boxes, and she would try to guess what they could have inside of them.

Other times, the humans would be celebrating. There would be men dressed in black, women dressed in white, and they would throw land flowers all around. Mara was always sure to grab the ones that fell into the water, so she could show them to her family.

Her favorite boats were the ones which carried animals. Some were large, and others were small. Some were covered in hair, just like the top of her head. Some were birds, like her seagulls, but with many colors. She longed to feed these types of birds, or for their feathers to fall down, so she could collect them.

Then one day, while she and her siblings were playing hide-and-seek, Mara spotted a small cave in a nearby ravine. They were swimming in deep waters, but the cave was up so high, it reached the surface. A waterfall poured down its mouth.

She knew her siblings would not find her, since none of them went above water like she did. She swam up and into the cave, making sure she could still see below for her siblings, but also sitting back far enough so they wouldn't easily spot her. She smiled to herself when she saw them swim right by without even looking up!

To pass the time, Mara began to braid her hair, which made her pet starfish wriggle around and tickle her. She also watched the seagulls in the sky. Mara wished she had some fish to feed them, but they kept her company nonetheless. Then, out past the waterfall, she noticed a large shadow. She peeked through the waters, and spotted the largest ship she had ever seen. It had sails of black, and from it came loud shouts and gun fire. Her seagull friends flew away as the sound carried over.

She knew immediately what it was – a pirate's ship!

Mara had heard many stories about pirates, but she had never seen one of their ships in real life. Part of her knew that she should stay hidden inside the cave, but another part of her wondered when she would ever see another pirate ship again. Curiosity grew inside of her like seaweed, and her heart began to sink as she watched the ship move further and further away.

Surely, it wouldn't hurt to have a closer look.

So, she swam after it. On the way over, she spotted her dolphin friends. She called out to them, but they refused to come. Having only her starfish perched in her hair, Mara approached the shadow of the pirate ship.

She peeked up above the surface, careful to keep most of her body hidden under the water. The waves were calm that day. However, the pirate ship was so big that it caused a great stir in its path. The current it caused grew, then it picked Mara up and swung her over. For a moment, she was in the air. She was so frightened and startled that she screamed. Her body landed hard on the nearby rocks.

This hurt Mara terribly, and she cried out once more. When at last she regained her balance, Mara realized that she could hear shouting. She looked up to see that the pirates were staring and pointing right at her.

She tried to crawl back to the water, but her bones and muscles ached from the fall, which made her move very slowly. This gave the pirates time to grab their nets and cast them down.

Mara was afraid. The nets clung to her skin and scraped at it, so much so that she began to bleed. She cried out for her family to come and find her, but they could not hear her under the waters. She cried out to her dolphin friends, but they kept their distance. Finally, she cried out to her seagulls, but they flew on into the sky.

Mara cried.

Once the pirates had her thrown onto the ship, they cast off the nets. They tied her to a pole where the sun hit her most. She could feel her skin start to dry out, which made her even weaker. Her starfish fell from her hair, and lay dying on the floor.

From the upper decks came a man dressed in red. Mara knew at once that he must be the captain. He looked down at her as if she were a prized fish to be hung on his walls.

"Brand her!" he yelled.

The other pirates cheered. They took out needles and gunpowder. Even though Mara was already tied up, they covered her mouth so she couldn't scream.

The captain came down to kneel before her. He pointed at her stomach, just below her navel.

"There!" he cried out. "Right there!"

The pirates brought their needles and gunpowder forward. They stabbed at her where their captain had instructed them to. The needles pierced deeply into her skin, causing her to bleed once more. There were so many needles that Mara couldn't count them all – to her, it only felt like one, giant cut along her abdomen.

It hurt worse than anything she had ever felt in her life. Even more than landing on the rocks. It was so painful that Mara thought she might die from it.

In her mind, she silently begged for someone to come and rescue her. She begged for a storm to come and sink the ship. But no one, and nothing, came to help.

So instead, she cried. Big tears spilled from her eyes as the pirates continued their work.

"Look at her!" they laughed. "Look at how she cries!"

The entire time, the captain stared down and watched.

When at last they were done, they untied Mara from the post. She tried to move away, but her body ached so much that she merely flopped over. The pirates pointed and laughed once more.

Finally, they picked her up and threw her back into the sea. The gush of water stung at her wounds. However, now that she was free, Mara at last saw what the pirates had done to her.

Along her stomach was a tattoo.

She immediately tried to rub it off with her hands, but that only agitated the wound, which caused her to bleed more. Mara became worried that sharks would smell the blood, so she rushed to grab some soft kelp to cover it.

She sat down to allow her wounds time to scab over. Periodically, she would lift up the kelp in order to check, silently wishing that the tattoo would wash off. Yet, every time she looked, she saw that it remained intact.

"What will I tell my family?" she cried out. "I cannot possibly keep this hidden forever!
Oh, how I wish there was a way to remove it! There must be something I can do to take it off!"

Her siblings, who believed that Mara was still playing hide-and-seek, heard her cries and swam to find her.

"Mara, we found you at last!" they exclaimed.

But Mara did not greet them happily. Instead, she brought her tail up and curled into it, so her torso and face were hidden. They asked her what was the matter, but she only shook her head. They tried to get her to leave and come back home.

Finally, her siblings left, and returned with their parents.

"Mara," said her mother. "What is the matter with you? It's not safe to be out alone like this, let's go home!"

Mara refused to budge.

"Mara!" her father yelled. "Do as your mother says, it's time to come home!"

He grabbed her by her arm and began to pull her away. As he did, she screamed out, and the kelp fell from her body. She tried to cover herself back up, but it was too late. Her whole family had already seen the tattoo across her.

"What is that?" her father asked, pointing at her. "Were you captured by pirates?"

They did not give her a chance to answer.

"Mara, how could you be so careless!" her mother went on. "We've told you so many times to stop watching the ships on the surface! Now look what's happened!"

"It wasn't us." her siblings said. "We didn't tell her to go to the surface! We were playing hide-and-seek but we didn't tell her where to hide!"

"Please, help me!" Mara began to cry again. "There must be some way to take it off! There must be a magic spell or something!"

"There isn't," her father answered. "We taught you better than this! You were careless, and now you must wear your shame, always!"

They tried to take her away once more, but Mara was so distraught that she fled into the dark waters.

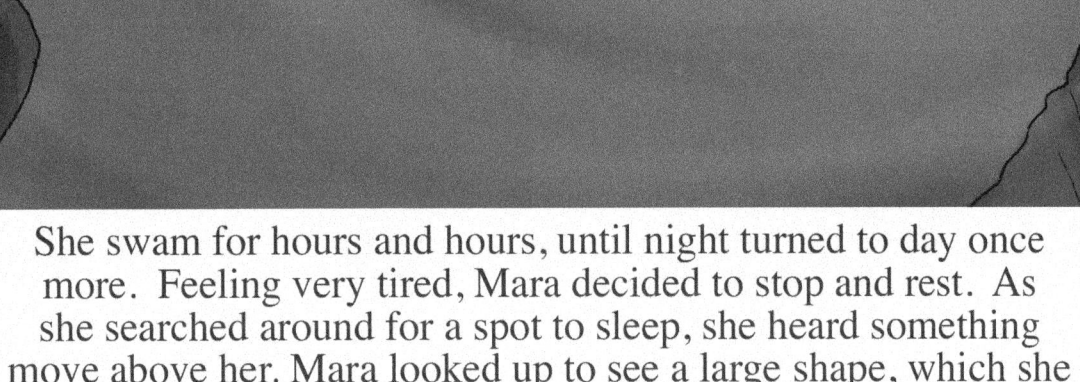

She swam for hours and hours, until night turned to day once more. Feeling very tired, Mara decided to stop and rest. As she searched around for a spot to sleep, she heard something move above her. Mara looked up to see a large shape, which she recognized to be a ship.

Immediately she was overwhelmed with fear so great, she thought she would faint. Instead, she took shelter behind large rocks.

Mara found herself having difficulty breathing, as if someone were holding their hands over her gills. Her heart beat fast, and everything around her was spinning. She didn't understand what was happening to her – was she drowning? Was that possible for a mermaid to do?

She wanted to look up to see if the ship had passed, but she could not bring herself to do it. In her head, she could hear the pirates laughing at her, and the tattoo across her body began to sting once more.

Mara waited in that spot for a very long time. As her breathing returned to normal, she began to wonder, "Would things always be like this? Just yesterday I was excited to spot a ship. How can something that once made me happy now be so terrifying?"

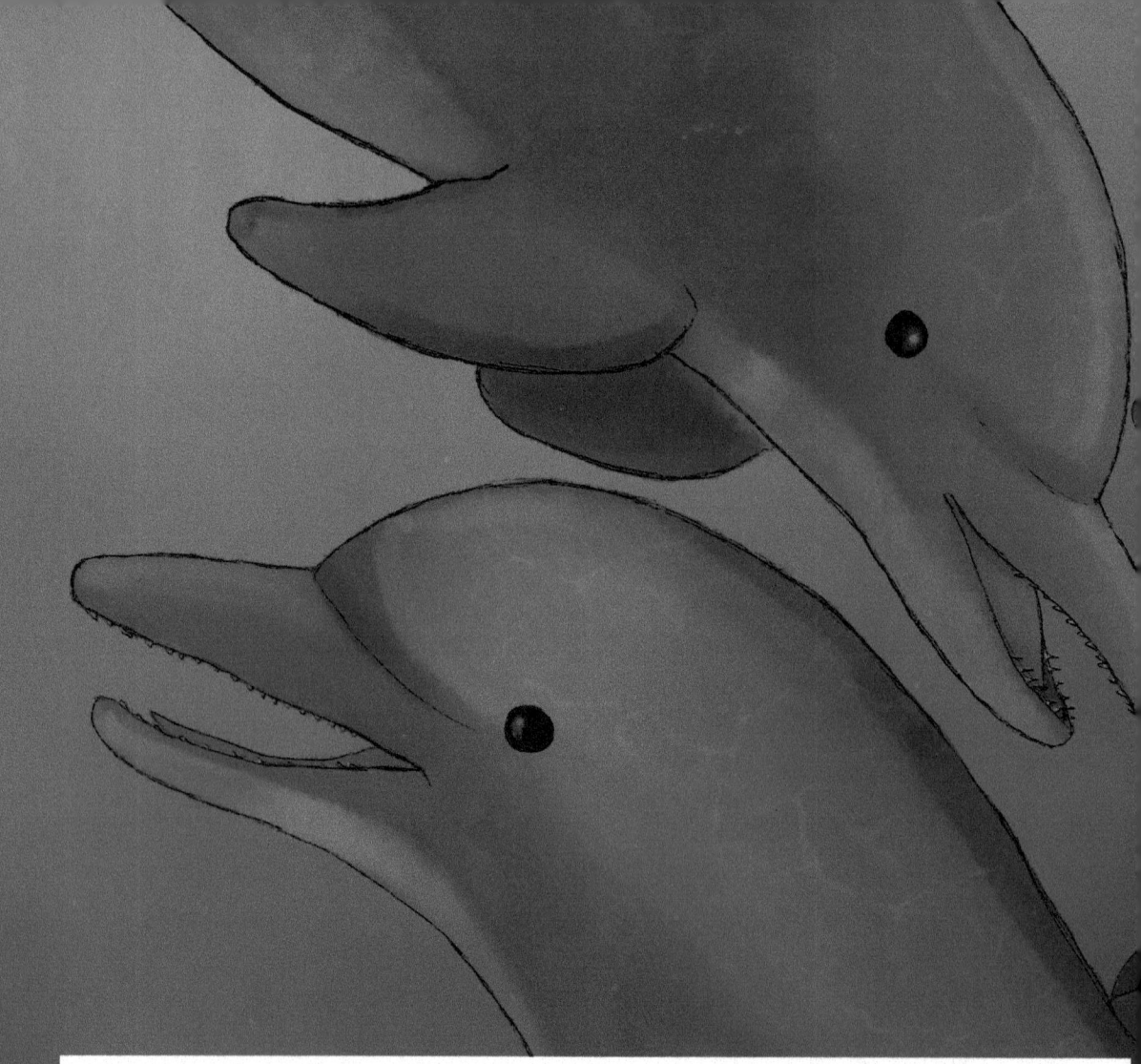

At this point, Mara's tattoo no longer bled. It had scabbed over. She sat down and picked at it. This hurt, but at the same time, it strangely felt good. When she picked at her skin, flecks of the tattoo came off as well. This started to leave behind a scar.

Mara thought that she would rather return to her family with scars over a tattoo.

Once she had determined this, she sought to find a way to carve the tattoo off of her body. As she swam along, Mara came across a pair of dolphins. It did not take her long to determine that these were her friends. She called out to them, and they rushed over to her. However, instead of coming to play or aid her in the journey, the two began to snap their jaws at her.

"Friends!" she cried out. "It is me, Mara!"

They did not listen, and instead continued to try and bite at her. Mara looked down at herself, and realized that her tattoo was bleeding again. On top of that, she still carried the smell of the pirates on her. The dolphins could not determine if she was prey or enemy, but one thing was for certain. They no longer recognized her.

Upon realizing the danger her life was in, Mara was quick to swim away into higher waters.

Eventually, Mara came across a cave, similar to the one she had hid in when she had spotted the pirate ship. Except instead of a waterfall, this one came with seals. They barked and snapped at Mara, but unlike the dolphins, they did not approach closer. Instead, they fled to higher parts of the island.

Mara peered around, wondering if any of the rocks around her were sharp enough to pierce into her skin. She reached out her hands and ran them along the walls. Suddenly, she brushed up against something so cold it stung.

Mara pulled back her hand, and realized her fingers were cut. She inspected the spot where she had been touching, and saw that wedged deep into the rocks was an abandoned knife.

Without hesitating, Mara took a firm grip on the handle and yanked it out. She looked over its blade, how rusted it had become from years of neglect. More than anything, Mara couldn't ignore the fact that a knife such as this had most likely been left behind by a pirate.

"How fitting," she thought to herself. "You were left to rot, same as I. And how fitting that now, you will make things right."

Mara put her back to the wall and lined up the knife alongside her tattoo. She wondered if she should pick in slow, shallow bits as she had done with her own fingernails, or see how far she could peel before the skin broke. Ultimately, she decided to go ahead and proceed, certain that she would be able to see which method would prove more effective.

As she sank the knife into her flesh, blood immediately started to pour out into the waters. It hurt so terribly that she screamed once again. She thought of how the pirates had laughed at her, how they had mocked her tears when she cried.

But then she thought about how angry her family had been with her, and how her friends no longer knew who she was, and Mara pressed on.

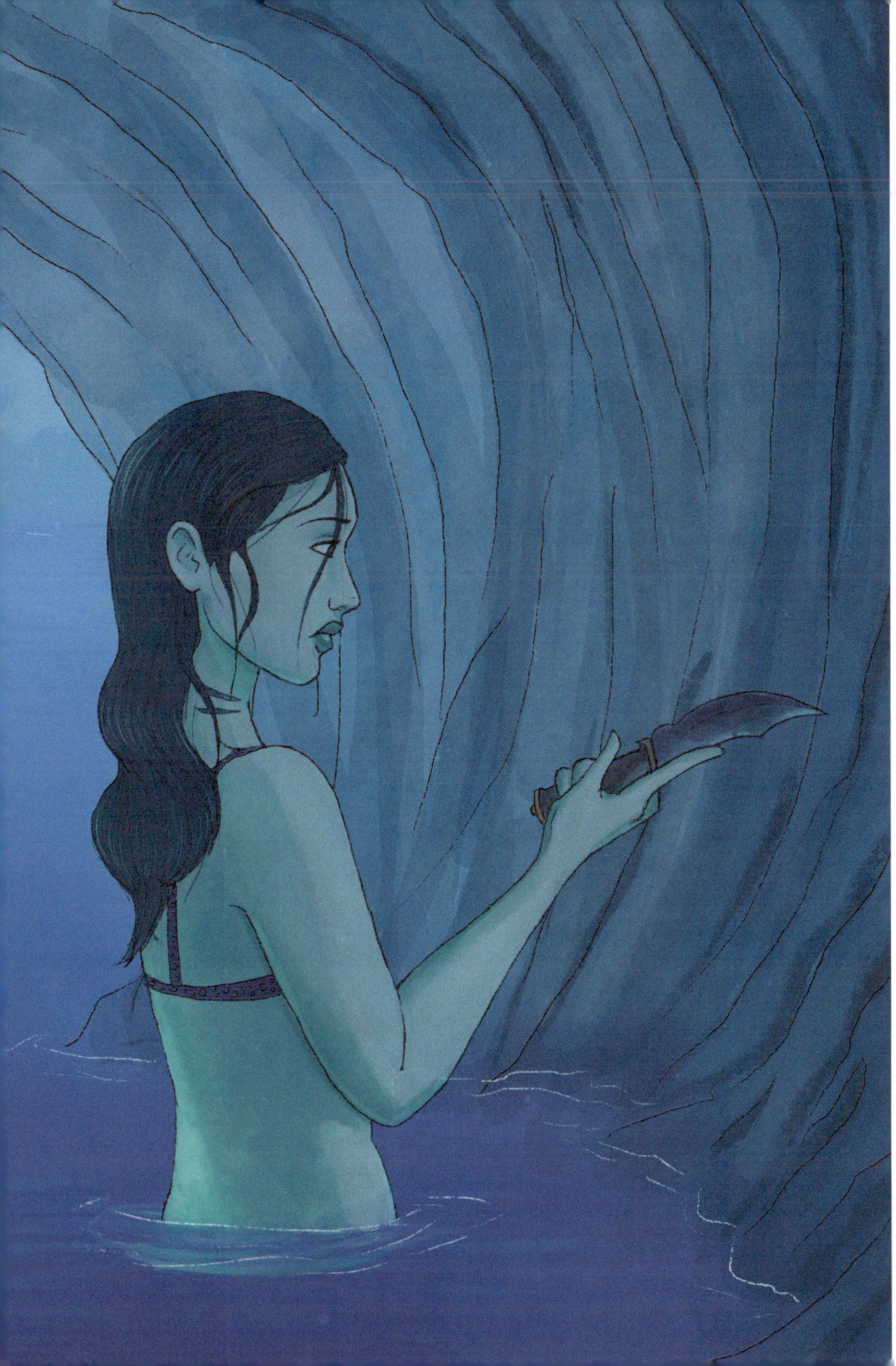

Mara had not gotten very far in her work before she noticed a large shadow swimming just outside the cave. At first, she thought she had imagined it,
but then the shadow returned, and even closer. That was when the top fin pierced through the water, and Mara knew at once that she had attracted the attention of a shark.

But Mara was not afraid. In fact, she welcomed the presence of this new predator. Unlike her friends, this shark didn't fear her. And unlike her friends, if this shark took a bite from her, it would not be a betrayal. In fact, if the shark bit in the right spot, it might swallow her tattoo whole.

Mara allowed the shark to swim up to her, its jaws open wide.

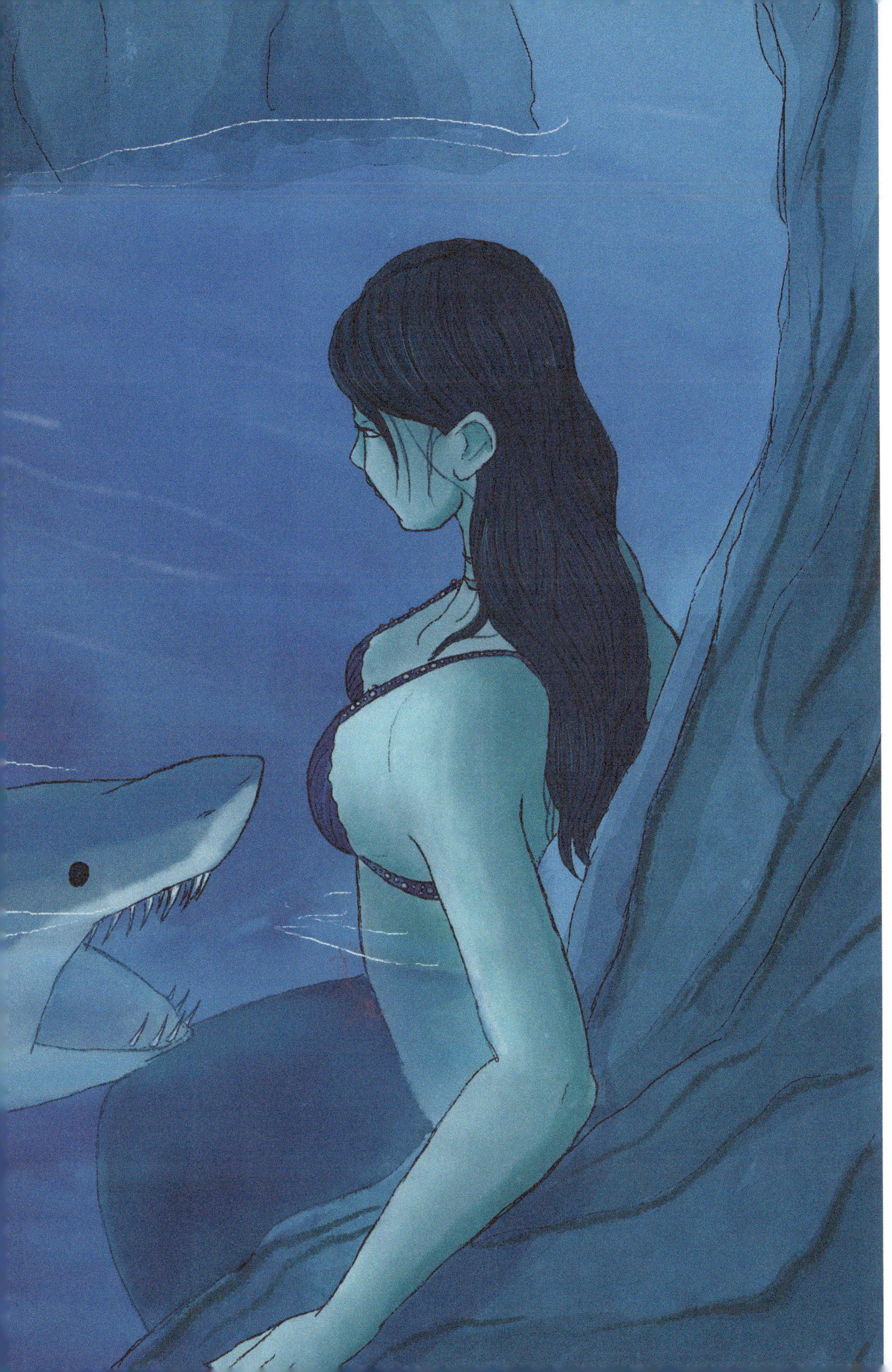

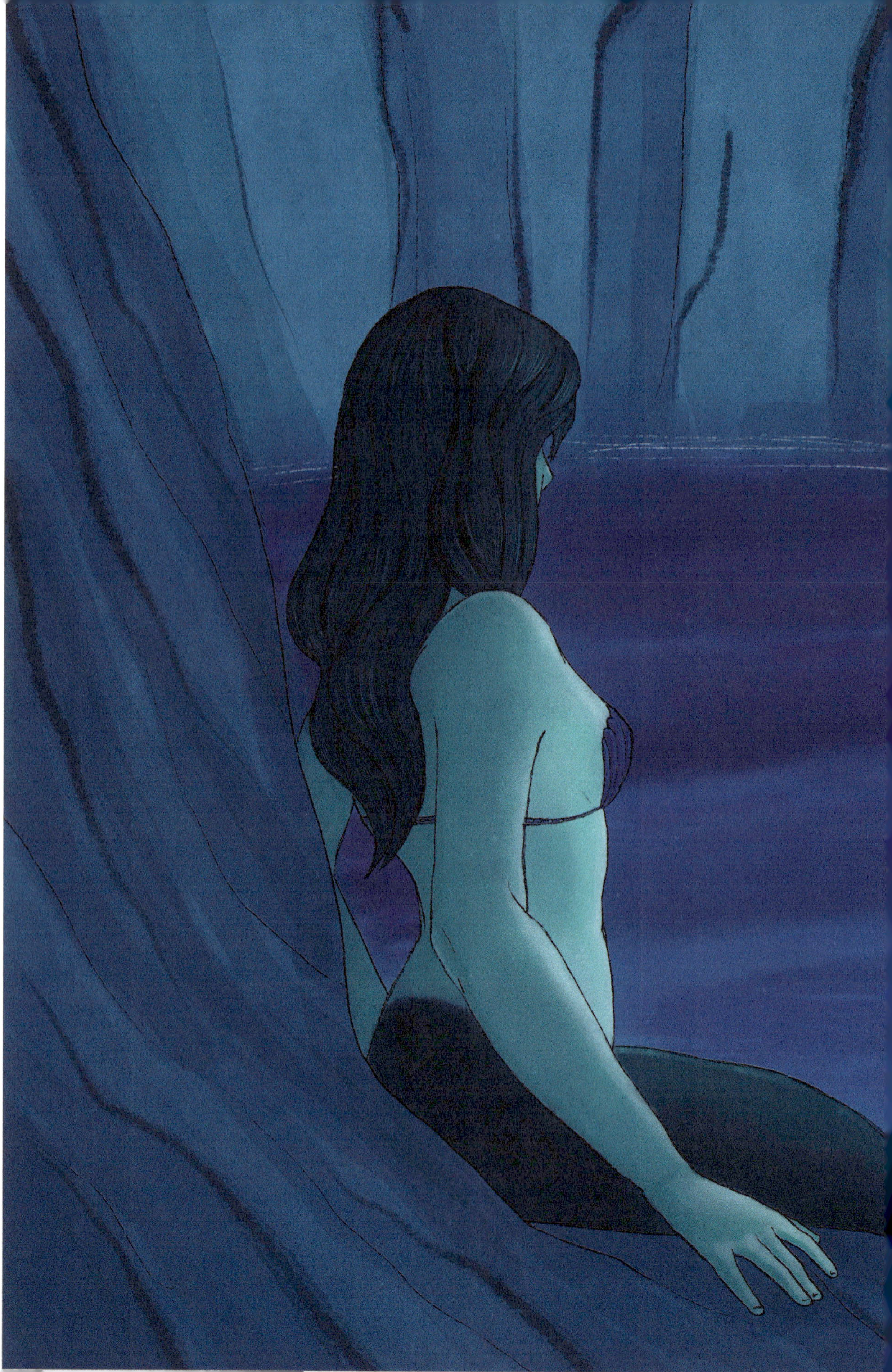

Just as it was about to take the first bite, however, Mara heard a loud splash. She opened her eyes to see that something was wrestling with the shark. She watched in awe as she realized her savior was a young merman.

He gripped at the shark's throat and forced it to turn around, until he was able to shove it out of the cave's mouth. Even with Mara's blood still fresh in the water, the shark swam off into the distance.

Once the two were alone, the merman focused his attention on Mara. His gaze was so intense that at first it frightened her. Then, she got a good look at him, and saw that across his chest was a tattoo.

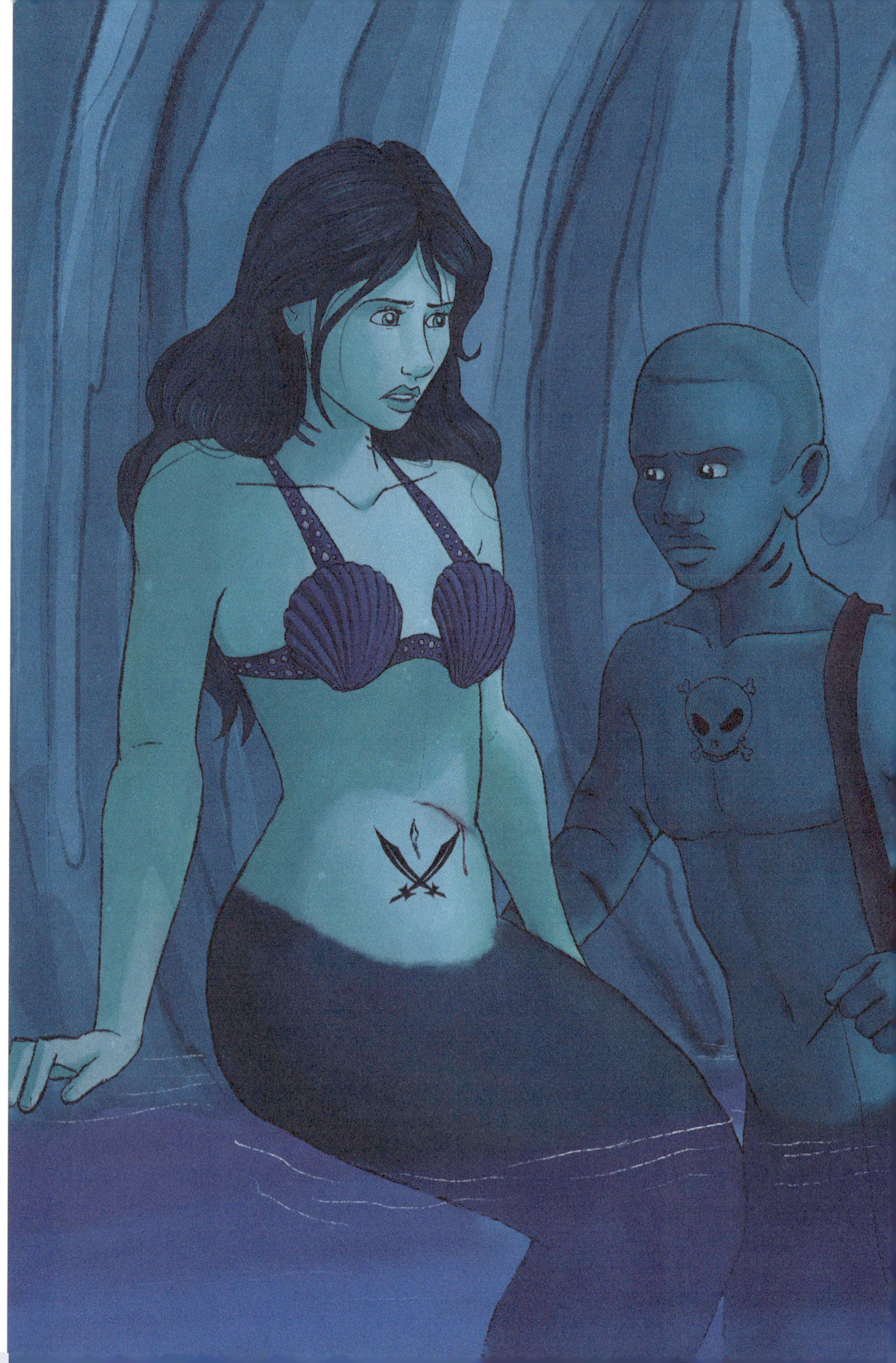

The merman placed his hands on Mara's wound. "We need to stop the bleeding." He said. That was when she noticed he was wearing a satchel across his waist. He reached into it and produced a needle and thread.

Mara gasped at the sight of the needle. She found it difficult to breathe once more, and everything started to spin.

"No!" she cried. "Don't!"

"I know it will hurt," he replied. His voice was so quiet and calm, as if this were not the first time he had said these words. "But, it's the only way."

"I don't want to stop!" Mara yelled. "I want this tattoo off of me!"

"You can't." The merman showed her his arms, which were covered in scars and ink.

Mara momentarily let go of her fears. She wanted to ask what had happened to the merman that his body had ended up in such a way. But she had a feeling that their stories were very similar, deeper still, she had a feeling that he might not want to share it just yet.

So instead, she asked him for his name.

"It is Cody," he answered.

Mara allowed Cody to stitch up her wound. It did indeed hurt, and there were many times when she was tempted to ask him to stop, but, when he finished, she was no longer bleeding. Then, the two merpeople sat there, unsure of what to do next.

Mara did not know where to go. She would not be welcomed back with her family as long as she had this tattoo, but if what Cody said was right, then there was no way to take it off.

"Where do you live?" she asked.

"East," he answered. "You can stop by sometime if you like. There are others like us who live there."

Mara thought about a place full of merpeople with tattoos. But instead of comfort, she just felt sad. How many had been captured by pirates as she had? How many more would this happen to?

"Cody," she began. "Why did this happen to us?"

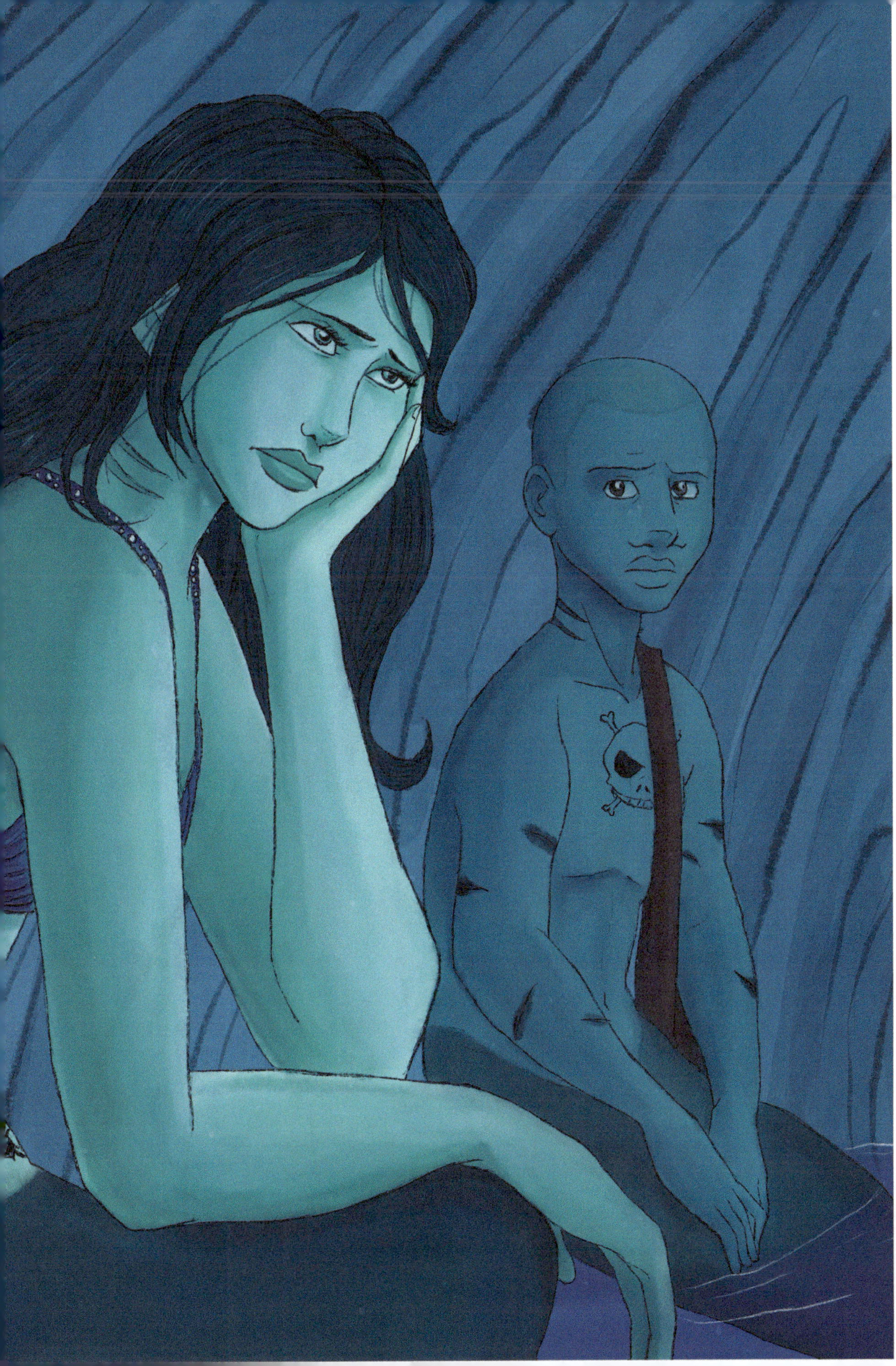

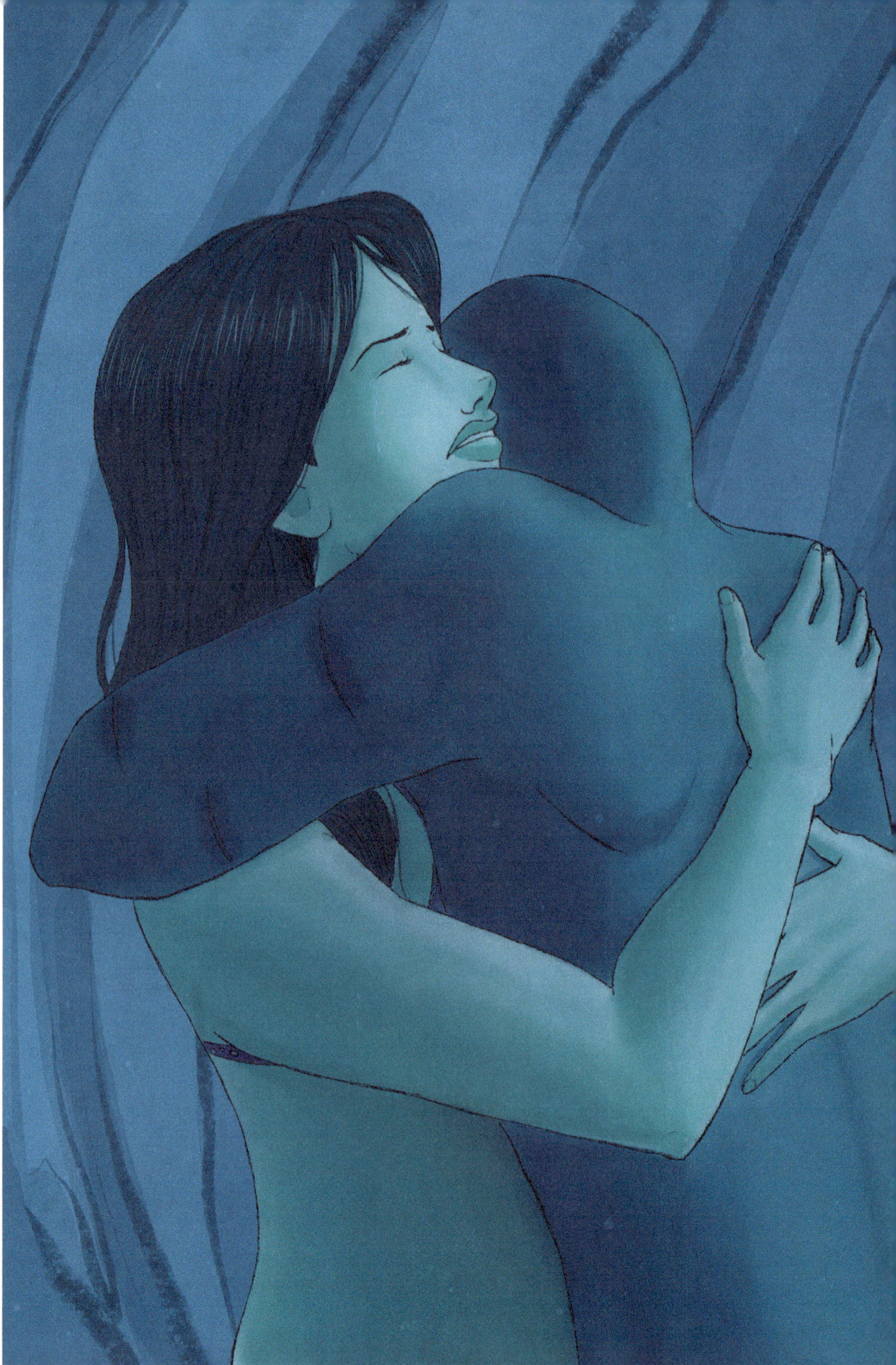

"There is no greater wisdom or reason." Cody said. "It was just something that happened. It is something that happens everyday. It is something that has happened before you, and will continue to happen long after you. But you are still here, and you are still you."

"I don't feel like myself anymore." Mara admitted. It was true, she could no longer go back to being that carefree mermaid who spent her days playing and watching ships. Even if her friends and family overcame their judgment, even if the tattoo was magically removed, she would always remember the experience.

"I know," said the merman. "And that may never go away. You know the world now in a way which not everyone can understand. But you are far from alone."

Mara wanted to argue, but at that moment she looked at the tattoo on Cody's chest, and the scars on his arms. She wondered how his family had reacted to the first, the second, and so on. She wondered how many nights he had spent alone, until he had found refuge among other tattooed merpeople. And she wondered how long it had taken before someone had sat down to tell him that everything was going to be alright.

Mara didn't say another word. She opened her arms, and upon seeing the invitation, Cody embraced her. The two new friends held on tightly to one another, and for the first time since she had been branded with the tattoo, Mara felt the slightest bit of hopefulness.

Cody took her back to his home, where Mara met his other friends. True to his word, they all came with a variety of tattoos. Some had one, like Mara, others had two, and others had several.

They did not ask her to share her story right away, instead they welcomed her in. They showed her around, and offered her some of their food.

They talked about the kind of games they liked to play, and the songs they liked to sing. They shared stories of their lives, the adventures and fun they had experienced over the years. Mara smiled and laughed, happier than she thought she would ever be again.

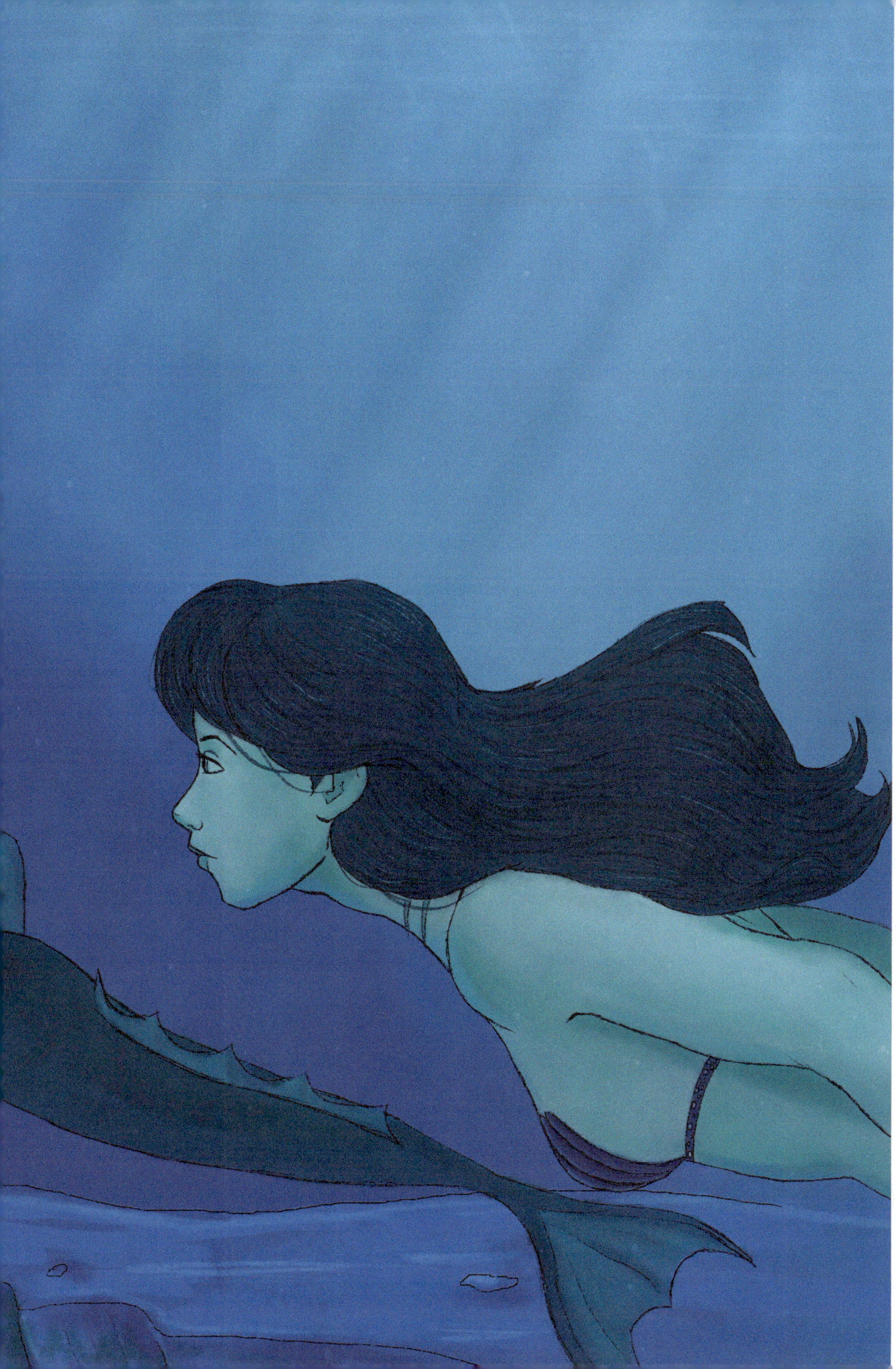

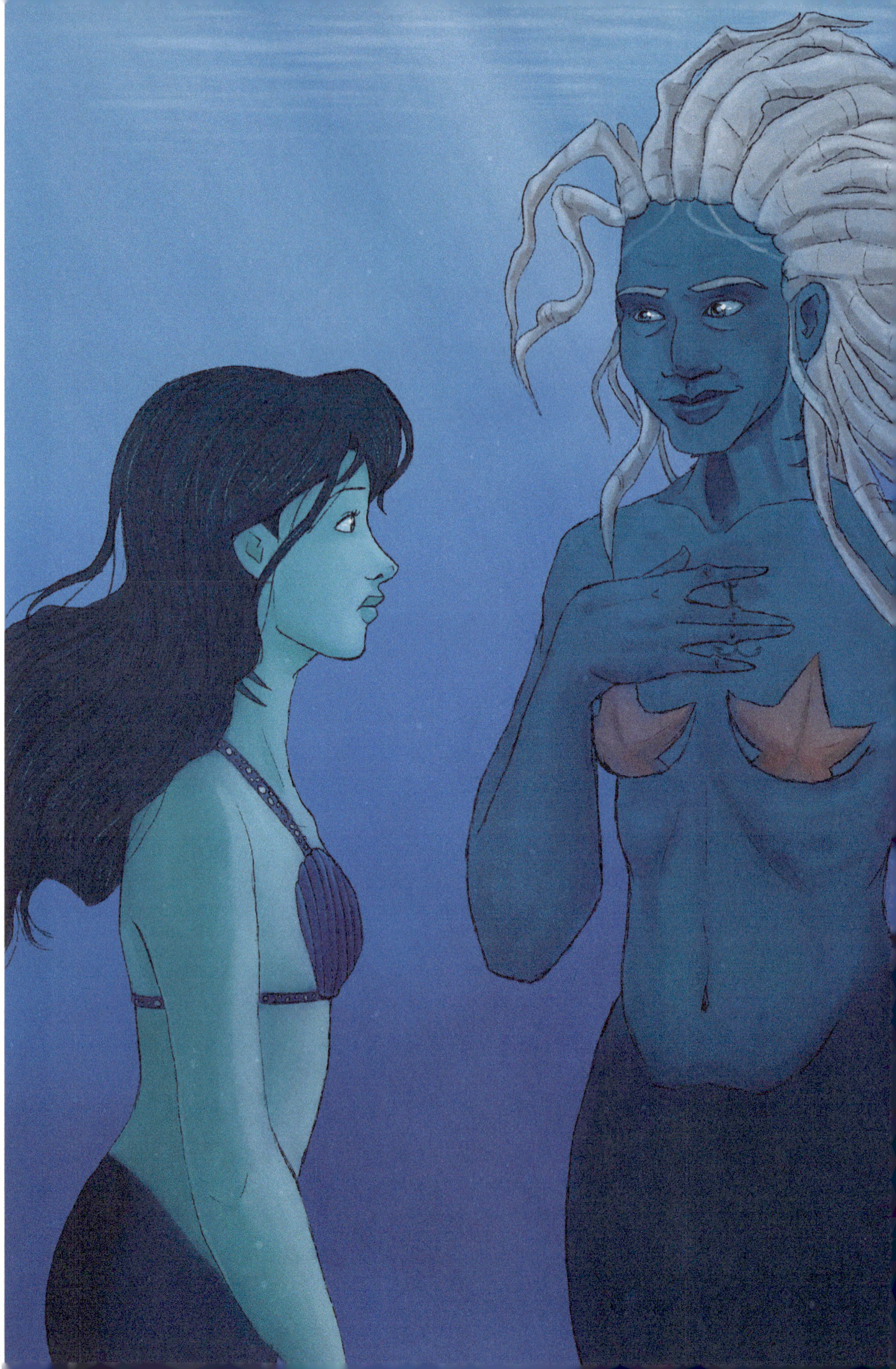

That evening, an older mermaid approached her. This one had two tattoos — one on her chest, the other on her shoulder. The tattoo on her shoulder intrigued Mara, because it was the image of a bird with a teardrop in its eye. She could not imagine pirate branding with such gentle imagery.

The older mermaid sensed Mara's curiosity. She pointed at the one on her chest. "I got this tattoo from pirates, but this tattoo," she pointed to the bird on her shoulder. "I gave to myself."

"Why?" Mara asked.

The older mermaid shrugged. "It is my body. I needed a reminder of that."

Mara stayed with these merpeople for the rest of her life. They traveled around the seven seas, telling others their stories about the tattoos. On occasion, they would find new merpeople with tattoos — some of them were freshly branded, and others had been alone for quite some time. They always offered a spot in their group, which some were happy to join, but others found contentment in where they were.

Mara shared her story many times, with anyone who she thought it would help to hear. She often helped other merpeople the same way Cody had saved her the first day they met.

She never learned how to remove her tattoo, nor did she feel any love for it. But it was a part of her, just like the scar she had when she attempted to cut it off.

Mara knew that her body was her own, and that she was herself.

The End